J SENDAK
Sendak, Jack.
The happy rain.
33277002724552

CAMAS PUBLIC LIBRARY

D1132875

WITHDRAWN

THIS BOOK WAS
PURCHASED WITH
GRANT FUNDS
FROM
TARGET®

THE
Happy Rain

THE
Happy Rain

by JACK SENDAK

PICTURES BY
MAURICE SENDAK

HARPER COLLINS   NEW YORK

Camas Public Library

TEXT COPYRIGHT © 1956 BY JACK SENDAK,

COPYRIGHT RENEWED 1984 BY JACK SENDAK

PICTURES COPYRIGHT © 1956 BY MAURICE SENDAK,

COPYRIGHT RENEWED 1984 BY MAURICE SENDAK

LIBRARY OF CONGRESS CATALOG CARD NUMBER: 56-8242

To my Father, and Mother

And my Sister, and Brother

1

THE people of Troekan were very fortunate. No other village could boast of such fine, glorious rain. Rain that flooded their gardens with a profusion of dazzling flowers. Rain that made music as it pattered on the tile roofs. Rain that perfumed the very air, drenched their clothes, and muddied their streets. It was a joy to live in Troekan.

Now, as this story begins, it was a typical day in the village of Troekan—a real soaker. Many of the villagers were picnicking in the country. Others were stretched out on the wet grass in the parks: airing their babies, listening to the band concert, or just napping.

School, which for reasons of health was held out-doors in the rain, had just been dismissed. And the children ran, shouting happily, past the shiny wet houses—toward the lake. It was just the right kind of a day for a swim.

In one of the houses, a mother's voice said, "What—Raymond and Yolande—still in the house on such a fine rainy day? Quick—out into the streets—or do I have to toss you both out of the window?"

Raymond and Yolande ran into the street, giggling. Mother was always joking.

"And, mind," she cried after them. "And, mind—you come back soaked to the skin—else I'll lock you both out."

Oh, of course Raymond and Yolande would get soaked to the skin, and muddy, and dirty. Didn't they every day? Playing their regular games of mud-rolling, puddle-jumping, and hide-and-splash?

Situated in the center of Troekan was the village square. As always, it was a hubbub of activity. Vendors were selling their soaking wares everywhere. The villagers were shopping, and discussing the affairs of the day. And they were forever arguing, and shouting, and laughing. While the children played games, or had mud-ball fights. And cried, and chased dogs, and ate. Everyone was having a grand time.

And above all the clatter and bustle could be heard the beautiful sound of the rain pattering on the tile roofs.

And, just as they did every night, everyone, including the children, stayed up as late as they wanted to. For there were so many things to do, and to see, and to hear. And, just as every day in Troekan, this one had been full of happiness, excitement, and fun.

As Raymond and Yolande prepared for bed, they were already making plans for the next day.

"We can dig a tremendous tunnel," said Yolande. "Right under the street—and we can make believe we are rabbits."

"Yes," added her brother, "and we can scare everybody that comes by."

Throughout the village everyone flung their windows wide open, the better to feel the rain as they slept. This, they believed, would assure them of fine dreams.

And soon the pattering rain soothed the villagers to sleep.

2

IN the middle of the night, a storm came up to rouse the people of Troekan. Starting with terrible suddenness, it mounted quickly to a great fury. Lightning tore through the darkened streets, and tremendous thunderclaps shook the houses. The pounding rain sounded like a million tomtoms. The wind, with fearful force, ripped the leaves from the trees and flung them about in wild confusion. What had been a peaceful, dreamy night became, now, a furious nightmare. The villagers shook in their beds.

When the morning finally came, the tempest ended and a silence that was even more terrible than the storm settled over the village.

In their room, Yolande whispered to her brother, "How very funny. You can't hear anything when it is so quiet. Not even the rain pattering on the roof."

"I think I am afraid," said Raymond.

"I'd be afraid, too, if I knew what there was to be afraid about. Go to the window, Raymond, and see what has happened."

"You go."

"Oh, Raymond. Boys are much braver than girls. Please go to the window."

"I don't feel very brave."

"Now, Raymond."

"Oh, all right—if I have to."

So Raymond tiptoed very slowly to the window, and, closing one eye, looked cautiously about with the other.

"Well? Well?" whispered Yolande. "Is there anything to be afraid about?"

"I—I think so."

"What is it?"

Raymond turned to look at his sister, and there were tears rolling down his cheeks.

"I think," he said, "I think it is the end of the world."

It had stopped raining.

3

CAN you imagine how it would be if the sun suddenly disappeared? Or if the moon disappeared? Or the stars? Or the sky altogether?

Well, so it was with the people of Troekan and their rain. There had never been a time in their entire history when it had ever stopped before. Not even for the smallest, smallest part of a second. They had never, ever thought that such a thing could happen. But now it had—and the people of Troekan were certain that it indeed was the end of the world.

How frightened they were. They shut their shutters tight. They shook with fear. And they wept, and they

8

wailed, and they wrung their hands. They kept their eyes tightly shut and huddled under the covers of their beds. Why, oh why, did such a thing have to happen to the happy village of Troekan!

But after several days of this the people of Troekan were worn out. They had no more tears to shed. Something more practical was needed now. Something would have to be done.

So, very carefully, notes were passed from house to house. And at last it was decided that they would all meet in the village square and make plans.

An awful sight greeted their eyes the next day, as they gathered in the square. The comforting dark clouds were gone; now there was only the harsh, glaring sun. And the soft, warm mud had become hard, and difficult to walk on. The dazzling flowers—all blown away. The trees—all bare. If the villagers had had any more tears left they could have certainly put them to good use now. Their hearts ached to see their village in such a state.

Very wisely, to protect themselves from the terrible sunny weather, most of the villagers carried umbrellas. And, of course, they had all muffled themselves up with all the clothes they could possibly wear.

Raymond and Yolande also came, walking sadly behind their parents. They, too, were all swaddled in protective clothing. Except, that is, for Yolande's hair, of which she was very proud. That hung down her back. And except for Raymond's nose, which was rather long and could not be completely covered.

Then one of the villagers, who was very fat, stepped forward and said, "People—people of Troekan. Something, yes indeed, something must be done. What good, now really, what good does it do us to sit in our homes and shake, yes, actually shake, with fear? No good at all. No good at all. It has stopped, yes, it has definitely stopped raining in Troekan. Well, let us make it start again."

The people of Troekan agreed.

"But how are we to do it?" they cried.

"What is to be done?"

"How are we to go about it?"

"What should we do?"

So the fat villager stepped forward once more and said, "Ah—that is, yes, that certainly is, indeed, a question."

The people of Troekan returned to their homes—to ponder on this question. How were they to make the rain fall again? They thought and they thought and they thought and they thought. In fact, they thought so hard and so long that their heads began to ache. And when, on the next day, they all assembled in the square again, they were just as puzzled as ever.

But a man, who was very thin, came forward and said, "I just thought of something—and I believe it is a good idea—and here it is. In our village—and such a sad village it is now—live three men—and one is a very wise old man—and one is a great scientist—and the other is an eminent philosopher—and this is my idea—and I think that it is a good one—and I believe that surely one of them must know how to make the rain fall—and why not ask them."

And as the thin man stopped to catch his breath, the people of Troekan cheered. Why not, indeed? It was a splendid idea.

First, they would ask the wise old man. He had lived for such a long time, and by now he knew the answers to almost anything. Quickly they decided to send a little boy, for they knew that the wise old man liked little boys. And of all the little boys in the village, they chose Raymond, because he had been the first to volunteer.

The wise old man was really very old—one hundred and seventy years old, to be exact. And he lived in a very old house. So old that all of it, except for the chimney, had crumbled away. But the old man loved his house so that he refused to move away. And he lived there still, alone, in the chimney.

When Raymond arrived at the old man's house, he found him standing on his head.

"Why are you standing on your head?" cried Raymond, astonished.

The wise old man grumbled—he did not like to be annoyed by people. But when he saw that it was a little boy who had asked him the question, he answered, in a feeble voice, "I have been standing on my feet for one hundred and seventy years—and they were beginning to grow tired. So now I am standing on my head, so as to give my feet a rest."

Raymond was delighted.

"What a wonderful idea," he said. "I'd love to stand on my head."

"My feet hardly hurt at all now."

"Really?"

"My head aches somewhat, though."

"I see. But the reason I came," said Raymond, "was to ask you how we can make it rain again."

"Everyone should stand on his head."

"What? . . . Will that make it rain?"

The old man didn't answer, but it seemed to Raymond that he nodded. It was hard to tell for sure, considering the awkward position he was in.

"Do you mean," persisted Raymond, "that if we all stood on our heads the rain would start falling?"

"Probably have to wear a hat, though."

"Oh, how really wise you are," said Raymond.

"Yes, yes," grumbled the wise old man, "probably need a hat." And with that, he went into his chimney and fell asleep.

When Raymond returned to the village square, he told the people of Troekan all that had happened.

What could it mean, they wondered. Was the wise old man talking about his aching feet—or was he indeed telling them how to make it rain? Must they stand on their heads?

"Yes, that is what we must do," said Raymond. "I was there and I should know. I asked the wise old man how to make the rain fall—and he said we should all stand on our heads. That is what he said. I heard it myself."

Well, then, if that is what they had to do to make it rain—then, that is what they would do. And so all the people of Troekan stood on their heads.

And they did everything standing on their heads. They went for walks—standing on their heads. They shook hands and said "How do you do" to each other —standing on their heads. And they carried their umbrellas—standing on their heads. And they ate their suppers—standing on their heads. It was all very unusual.

"It feels very funny to stand on your head," said Yolande to her brother. "It is as though the whole world was topsy-turvy."

"Yes, it does," agreed Raymond. "It is as though I was turning a somersault—and I got stuck halfway."

They both giggled.

But the people of Troekan were far from being amused. For three days they had balanced themselves precariously on their heads, and still there was no rain. So, again, they all gathered in the village square.

One of the villagers, who was very tall, came forward and said, "Uh, we have been on our heads, uh, so to speak, uh, for three days now. And, uh, in spite of some pretty sore heads, uh, there has been, uh, not a bit of rain. Uh, the wise old man might have been wrong. We, uh, should go to see the scientist, uh, and, uh, ask him what is to be, uh, done."

The villagers readily agreed to this and they sent a man with a beard, for they knew that the scientist liked men with beards, to ask him how they were to make it rain again.

When the man with the beard arrived at the scientist's house, he found it all locked up with nails, and chains, and boards, and bars on the windows. So, with the loudest voice he could manage, he shouted, and coughed, and called, and even whistled—until, finally, the scientist stuck his nose through one of the barred windows.

"Go away. Go away," he said fretfully. "Don't you come any closer to my house. It is full of secret and scientific inventions. You must not see them. They are secret. Secret. Secret. Go away."

But when the scientist saw that it was a man with a beard who had called, he became a little more friendly and said, "What can I do for you, old sir?"

So the man with the beard said, "It has stopped raining in Troekan. We would like to know how to make it start again."

"Hah," said the scientist. "A simple matter. But remember—don't you come any closer to my house. Full of secrets, you know. Wait—I shall come out."

And, in a little while, the scientist squeezed himself out of a secret door in the side of the house, pulling a strange-looking machine with him. The machine had all kinds of secret dials, switches, strings, and knobs.

Then the scientist started the machine. It made all kinds of secret noises, and did all kinds of secret things. The man with the beard was quite amazed. Whereupon the scientist nodded with satisfaction and dragged the machine and himself back through the secret door in his house. In a twinkling he was at the window again.

"Well, old sir," he said, "I have solved the problem. But first—must you stand on your head so? It makes me quite dizzy."

So the man with the beard said, "The wise old man said that if we would stand on our heads, it would rain."

The scientist laughed heartily at this.

"Such nonsense," he said. "Why, my machine told me why there was no rain. Listen carefully, old sir. What I am going to tell you is very secret and scientific stuff, and it may be a little difficult for you to understand. Are you listening carefully?"

The man with the beard nodded.

"Well, then," said the scientist. "You see, the rain comes from the clouds. Now, the holes in the clouds that the rain comes through have gotten all clogged up. You must make new holes in the clouds, and let the rain out. Simple, eh? Hah, we scientists are all very simple—secret and simple."

The man with the beard got back down on his feet and bowed before the great scientist.

"How marvelous," he said. "Why didn't we think of that? But—but—but how are we to make new holes in the clouds?"

"How stupid you are. Why, it is simple, old sir—secret and simple. Why, just get some cannons and shoot new holes in the clouds. Simple—simple—simple —simple—"

When the man with the beard heard this, he ran back to the square and related to the people of Troekan all that he had seen and heard.

The villagers were overjoyed. This was surely the answer. Why hadn't they thought of it? Quickly they sprang to their feet again and got together all the cannons they could find. And, before long, they were blazing away at the clouds.

The noise was deafening. The villagers had to shout to make themselves heard. Fathers had to roar at their children. Boys had to bellow at their friends. Girls had to yell at their dolls. Dogs had to howl at the cats. But, still, nothing could be heard—except the terrible noise of the cannons.

Also, the cannon balls that were fired at the clouds soon found their way back to earth, falling perilously close to the villagers. They had to keep dodging them, and this made them all terribly uneasy.

Raymond, though, was having a fine time. He was firing his slingshot.

"I wish I had one of those cannons," he said. "I don't think I can hit the clouds with this slingshot."

"I don't think the cannons are hitting the clouds either," said Yolande. "It hasn't started raining yet."

4

YOLANDE was right. The shooting of the cannons went on for three days, and all for nothing. For there was still no rain. The people of Troekan came to the village square again. They were all hoarse, a little deaf, and very unhappy.

A man, who was very short, climbed upon a large rock, coughed, cleared his throat, and when everyone had stopped talking, said, "The philosopher."

His speech, like his stature, was rather brief, but the villagers agreed that it would indeed be best to go to the philosopher. And, this time, they sent Yolande.

They knew that the philosopher liked little girls, and Yolande was the prettiest one in the village.

The philosopher lived in the forest—on a bearskin. That was his only home. Books, thousands of them, were scattered all over. They were on the grass, in the bushes, and stuck into hollows of the trees. Around the beloved philosopher sat many forest animals—eating the pages out of the books. The philosopher himself was sitting cross-legged on his rug, reading.

Yolande approached timidly and said, "Oh—oh—Mister Philosopher—"

The philosopher went on reading.

Yolande tried again.

"Please—Sir Philosopher. It has stopped raining in Troekan. Can you please tell us how to turn it on again?"

The philosopher went on reading, but then, when he saw that it was a little girl who had asked him the question, he smiled and said, "Rain—is it? I think I can coax the rain to fall. Such pretty long hair you have."

The philosopher then began to poke among his books and he picked out one that was tremendously big. He studied some pages and, after a few moments, sighed deeply and said, "Ah, here it is—right on this page. Is it not wonderful how we can find the answers to all our problems in these ancient books? Our ancient teachers knew the answers to everything. And today we can do nothing but follow their teachings—and wonder at their wonderfulness."

Yolande, not knowing exactly why, curtsied. The philosopher was so awfully smart.

"Yes," continued the philosopher. "Our ancient teachers—how wise they were. Now, to make it rain—one must put a paper bag over one's head."

"A paper bag?" cried Yolande.

The philosopher nodded profoundly.

"Why, of course—a paper bag. It says so—right here —see."

Yolande nodded, although she really didn't see at all. The print in the book was so tiny, and so faded, that she could not make out one word from the other. But she knew that if the philosopher said that it was there, then there it must be.

"This book," said the philosopher, "was written by an ancient teacher thousands of years ago. And to this day no one has dared to doubt a word he said. He says a paper bag over one's head will make the rain fall. So it must be. Why, here on these pages he lists all the things that a paper bag will cure. From head colds to sprained ankles. Truly remarkable."

Upon which, the philosopher and the friendly

forest animals went back to reading and eating the books.

Yolande raced back to the village square as fast as her little legs could carry her and told the people of Troekan all that she had learned. They were amazed when they realized that it took only a paper bag to make it rain. And there could be no doubt about it either. How could one dare doubt our ancient teachers? Before long, everyone was wearing the strange headdress.

Raymond and Yolande, too, wore the paper bags. And, just for fun, Yolande drew a picture on her bag of how she would like to look when she grew up. While Raymond, not to be outdone, drew a picture on his paper bag of how he would not like to look when he grew up.

Anyway, for three days this went on and the people of Troekan became rather tired of it all. Their knees and ankles were all barked from bumping into things, and their noses tickled. Yet, for all their trouble, there was not so much as a drizzle.

Back again to the village square they went, all feeling terribly sad. They had asked the three wisest men in the village how to make it rain. But the sun still shone. What were they to do now? They thought and they thought and they thought.

At last a man, who was very bald and who had not uttered a word during the entire affair, stepped forward and said, "We, the people of Troekan, have posed, have asked, have inquired, that is, have put queries to the three most learned, most wise, most well-informed men in the village. And still not an indication, not a hint, not a mark, that is, not a sign of rain. I have considered, given thought to this problem, and I think, I believe, am of the opinion that we should speak to, discuss, converse with our mayor. He is always solving, unraveling, finding the solutions of, that is, clearing up all sorts of problems. Perhaps he can get to the bottom of ours."

The people of Troekan thought this was an excellent idea and they sent a lady, for they knew that the mayor liked ladies, to ask him what should be done.

The mayor lived in a gigantic house, just filled with pencils and pens and erasers and letters and notebooks. The lady had to search through all the rooms until she finally found him. He was sitting at his desk, behind a stack of papers that reached almost to the ceiling.

When the lady knocked at the door, the mayor cried, "Leave me alone. Do leave me alone. Can't you see that I am busy? So busy. Busy. Busy. I have so much to do. Go away. I am so busy."

But when he saw that it was a lady who was calling, he hopped off his stool, rubbed his hands, beamed happily, and said, "Ah—dear lady. What can I do for you?"

And the lady answered, "Oh, mayor, it has stopped raining in Troekan. We have gone to the wise old man and he told us to stand on our heads. But there was no rain. Then we went to the scientist and he told us to shoot cannon balls at the clouds. But that did not help either. So we went to the philosopher and he told us to cover our heads with paper bags. Still there was no rain. What are we to do, mayor? We must have our beautiful rain back again."

The mayor rubbed his hands.

"No rain in Troekan, eh? I hadn't noticed. I have been so busy, you know. No rain, well, well."

The mayor wrinkled his brow, to show the lady that he was thinking very hard. He rubbed his hands some more, and then he began hopping up and down.

"I have it, dear lady," he cried. "You went to the three wisest men in the village, and what they told you must be true. For, you must admit, they are never wrong—which, to carry the point further, must mean that they are always right. I think, then, that the fault must lie with you people of Troekan. For if the three wise men are right, then somebody else must be wrong. Do you follow me?"

"I think so," answered the somewhat puzzled lady.

"Well, then," continued the mayor, "I believe you must do what the three wise men told you to do—all at once. Yes, you must stand on your heads, shoot cannon balls at the clouds, and wear those paper bags. Then you will have rain. No doubt about it. No doubt about it. I am right. You will have your rain."

Then the mayor hopped back on the stool, allowed the lady to kiss his cheek, and busied himself once more with his papers.

The lady hurried back to the village square to tell all the people the good news.

5

IF a traveler from some far-off village had happened upon Troekan that day, he would have thought that they must certainly have all gone mad. For a sight of the greatest confusion would have greeted his eyes. He would have seen the people of Troekan, standing on heads that were hidden by paper bags, shooting cannon balls at the sky.

The villagers themselves, though, did not think they were the least bit mad. They were all of the firm conviction that the rain would soon be pattering away merrily on their tile roofs. Hadn't the mayor said so? There could be no doubt of it, he had said. And the villagers had none. They even threw their umbrellas away.

But after three days, when their heads ached from standing on them, when their throats were sore from shouting above the noise of the cannon, when they were hurting from the bruises of bumping into things —the people of Troekan lost all hope. It did not rain.

They gave up. There was nothing else to do. They ran back to their homes. They huddled under the covers of their beds. And they wept, and they wailed, and they wrung their hands. They had failed. There was nothing else to do now but weep.

In their room, Raymond asked his sister, "What are we to do now?"

"Spend the rest of our lives in bed," said Yolande.

"But, Yolande, I wouldn't want to do that."

"There is nothing else to do when it is the end of the world."

They were silent for a while, then Raymond said, "We used to have so much fun. Let's pretend it is raining."

"I don't want to pretend," pouted Yolande. "I want it really to rain."

"Oh, so do I," wailed Raymond.

Whenever Yolande thought very hard, she chewed on the knuckles of her left hand. It always helped her to think better. That was what she was doing now, and Raymond waited hopefully.

At last, Yolande said, "We must tell the clouds we want rain."

"Yes," said Raymond. "But the three wise men and the mayor—"

But Yolande was not listening—she went on chewing her knuckles and thinking aloud.

"How can the clouds know that we want rain if we never, ever told them so? Of course, we stood on our heads. Now, we knew that was supposed to bring the rain—but did the clouds know? And when we shot cannon balls at them, what could they think but that we were trying to drive them away forever? The poor clouds, we have been so mean to them. And even though the paper bags must surely cure head colds and sprained ankles—still, the clouds might have thought that we didn't even want to look at them. We never told them we wanted rain. How were they to know? Oh, Raymond," Yolande suddenly cried. "We must tell them. We must tell them. But how—how?"

Raymond brightened. Yolande was finished thinking and now he could join the conversation. It was such a strain not to talk.

"Maybe," he said, "if I got my balloon I—"

But Yolande interrupted.

"Balloon? Raymond, that is just the thing. I can write the message and put it in a bottle—they always send messages in bottles—and, then, we can tie it to the balloon, and away it will fly to the clouds. Oh, Raymond, how clever you are."

Joyously, she kissed him, and Raymond glowed with happiness because he had been so helpful.

Meanwhile, several of the villagers who were not weeping in bed were busily gathering wood for the purpose of boarding up the windows and doors of their homes. They would have to spend the rest of their lives indoors. Their homes, thus, would stand impenetrable against the blazing sun. The villagers, inside, could be well protected as they were bewailing their fate. There was really nothing else to do in the face of the terrible calamity that had befallen them. Everyone agreed to that. Might as well last out the calamity as best they could.

But the excited cries of Raymond and Yolande soon had them all running from every direction.

"What is it? What new misfortune has happened now?" they cried.

Yolande tried to reassure them.

"No misfortune at all," she said. "My brother and I have sent a message to the clouds."

The villagers looked at each other in puzzlement.

This was all very strange.

"What on earth for?" they wanted to know.

So Raymond and Yolande said that they had realized that the clouds did not understand that the people of Troekan wanted rain. They had realized that the clouds must think that the villagers did not want them any more. And they told the villagers that they had sent the message in a balloon.

The people of Troekan marveled at the wisdom of the two children.

"Why," said some, "they are wiser than the wise old man."

"Wiser, even," said others, "than the scientist." ·

And the men of the village declared in loud voices, "Much wiser than the philosopher, to be sure."

And the women shouted, in turn, "Or the mayor, too, for that matter."

Raymond and Yolande blushed with happiness over such praise. And their parents were so proud of them they kissed them and hugged them over and over again.

Joy once more filled the hearts of the people of Troekan. The boarding up of the homes was put off for a while. With the balloon, flying bravely toward the clouds, went all the hopes and the prayers of the townspeople.

"But—what was the message you sent?" asked one of the villagers.

And Yolande, her long hair ruffled by the same breeze that was speeding the balloon aloft, replied, "I wrote: REALLY—REALLY—WE DO LOVE YOU."

6

THE next two days were filled with feverish excitement. Would the balloon reach the clouds? Or would it not?

Three men were posted on three of the many tile roofs of Troekan. With the aid of three huge spyglasses, they reported to the others the progress of the balloon. Was it still going up? Was it coming down? Was it lost? Was it found? All these questions the three watchers had to answer, keeping always an eye on the soaring balloon. They did a heroic job.

Time after time the balloon ran into difficulties, only to be saved just at the right moment. Once, when

it began to fall like a stone, a sudden burst of wind
sent it upward again just as it was about to crash.
Then, when a hawk swooped to attack it, a lightning
bolt singed his feathers and frightened him off. And,
when the balloon seemed ready to burst from the heat
of the sun, big black clouds rolled in and made everything right.

But, on the morning of the third day, the precious
balloon disappeared altogether.

"Could it have finally reached the clouds?" wondered some of the villagers.

"Maybe it burst," worried the others.

The three men on the three tile roofs squinted with
all their might into the three spyglasses—to no avail.
The balloon was never more seen.

"Do you think an eagle ate it up?" asked Raymond.

Yolande did not answer. She just stared up at the
sky, chewing the knuckles of her left hand.

There was no rain that day. The people of Troekan
walked sadly back to their homes.

"Tomorrow we will board up the windows and
doors," muttered the men among themselves.

"Tomorrow we will start weeping again," said the
women.

7

THERE was very little sleep that night. A mysterious wind came up to rouse the villagers. The houses creaked and groaned as the wind whipped eerily through the dusty streets. And the trees, stretching their bare limbs, seemed to be shaking themselves awake. The villagers huddled fearfully in their beds.

When morning finally came, the people of Troekan heard another sound—a strange sound. Like a tap-tap-tapping. What new dreadful thing could have occurred now?

Raymond peered cautiously, with one eye shut, out of the window.

"Is it something to be afraid of?" whispered Yolande.

Raymond gave a cry of joy—a cry that was soon to be repeated throughout the entire village.

"Don't you know what that tapping is?" he shouted, trying to laugh and cry at the same time. "Why, it is rain—falling on our tile roofs. It is the end of the end of the world."

The people of Troekan, as you can well imagine, went wild with joy. Their days of fear and heartbreak were over. It was raining again in Troekan. Their happy, glorious rain.

And was it Raymond and Yolande who had accomplished this miracle for them? Could it indeed have been the message they had sent?

"Of course not," said some skeptics. "The balloon had nothing to do with it. Probably would have rained anyway."

But the great majority of the villagers would not agree to this.

"We had tried so many ways to make the rain fall," they said. "And they all ended in failure. While now, just as the balloon disappeared, the rain returned."

Raymond and Yolande became the greatest heroes that Troekan ever had. A statue of them, and the precious balloon, would be made and placed in the village square. Hundreds of gifts, everything you could think of—toys, candy, clothes—were showered upon them. It was like a dream come true for the happy little brother and sister.

And they had a glorious celebration that day—as the cooling Troekan rain drenched their clothes, muddied their streets, and nourished the young seedlings of the soon-to-be-growing plants. Everyone was there. Everyone, that is, except for the wise old man, who would not leave his adored chimney. Or the scientist, who was afraid to come lest someone steal his secrets. Nor was the philosopher there, for he was far too engrossed in reading his musty books. And the mayor was so busy writing a speech for the occasion that he just did not have time to come. But everyone else was there—and they all had the most wonderful time you could ever imagine.

And, because it rained happily ever after, the people of Troekan lived happily ever after.